To the Ashes

First published 1980 by Jonathan Cape Ltd
This edition published 2014 by Walker Books Ltd, 87 Vauxhall Walk, London SE11 5HJ

2 4 6 8 10 9 7 5 3 1

Text © 1978 the Estate of Russell Hoban • Illustrations © 1980 Quentin Blake

This book has been typeset in Bembo

Printed in China

British Library Cataloguing in Publication Data:
a catalogue record for this book is available from the British Library

ISBN 978-1-4063-5820-9

www.walker.co.uk

The Twenty-Elephant Restaurant

Russell Hoban & Quentin Blake

WALKER
BOOKS

A man and a woman lived in a little house. They had a
bed and a table and two chairs. The bed was good and
the chairs were good but the table wobbled. The man
always had to put a book of matches under one leg,
sometimes under two. After a while the matchbooks
would disappear and he would have to get new ones.

When Christmas came, the man gave the woman a handkerchief and she gave him a tie. They sat down at the table and said, "Merry Christmas."

"It doesn't feel like Christmas," said the woman.

"No wonder," said the man.

"What do you mean?" said the woman.

"This table," said the man.

"What about the table?" said the woman.

"It's wearing me out," said the man.

The woman shook her head. All day she walked around shaking her head.

That evening at supper the man said to her, "Why are you shaking your head?"

"It isn't right," she said. "It's wrong."

"What's wrong?" he said.

"The way things are with you and that table," said the woman. "It's all right for a man to wear out a table, but a table shouldn't wear out a man."

"It was just a manner of speaking," said the man. "I didn't really mean that the table is wearing me out."

"I've been thinking about it all day," said the woman. "Before we got that table you were young and handsome. Now you're old and ugly. What you said was true. That table is wearing you out."

"But we've had that table for fifty years," said the man. "It stands to reason I'm not as young and handsome as I was fifty years ago."

"Whether it stands to reason we don't know," said the woman. "All we know is how it was before the table and how it is now."

"What do you think I should do?" said the man.

"It isn't for me to say," said the woman.

"Say it anyhow," said the man.

"I think you should make a new table," said the woman.

"Make one?" said the man. "I've never made a table. We bought the old one."

"Look at the wrapped bread they sell nowadays," said the woman. "Look at the chemicals they put in chickens. Look at pollution. How can you expect to buy a good table?"

"You're right," said the man. "I'll find a tablewood

tree and I'll cut it down and saw it up and I'll make a new table."

"I'm glad you've decided to do that," said the woman. "I think that's a wise decision."

The man went into the woods and found a good straight-grained tablewood tree. He cut it down and sawed it up. He stacked the wood and left it to season for a couple of years.

Every so often he turned it over so that it would not warp. He could hardly wait to make the table, and when the wood was well seasoned he measured it off and sawed it to size. He drilled holes and pegged it together and made the table. He planed it smooth and he sanded it down and there it was, a new table.

"That really is a young, handsome, strong new table," said the man. "The old table was wearing me out, but this one is building me up."

"You look much better," said the woman. "You look fifty years younger already. There's nothing like a new table."

"You're absolutely right," said the man. "And that table is really strong. It's steady as a rock. No matchbooks under that table. Elephants could dance on that table."

"How many?" said the woman.

"Only one, really," said the man. "I don't think there's room for two."

"Oh," said the woman. "When you said elephants, I thought you meant more than one."

"One to a table, I'd say," said the man. "I could make more tables for that matter. There's lots of wood left from the tree I cut down."

"Where would we get the elephants?" said the woman.

"Advertise in the Classified Section," said the man. "Elephants wanted for table work. Must be agile."

"Then we'd have to pay them," said the woman.

"If people paid to see them dance, then we could pay the elephants," said the man.

"How do you know they'll be worth paying to see?" said the woman. "Maybe they won't be good dancers."

"We could open a restaurant," said the man. "The elephants could wait on the tables, and in their spare time they could practise dancing until they're good enough so people will pay to see them."

"They'll need a dancing instructor," said the woman.

"We can work it out as we go along," said the man. "The first thing is more tables." He measured and sawed and drilled and pegged and planed and sanded night and day, and he made seventeen more tables, all of them as strong and steady as the first one and none of them needing matchbooks under the legs.

When he'd made the tables, he couldn't get them all inside the little house. Even with tables standing on top of tables, seven of them had to wait outside.

"A tent?" said the woman.

"Elephants and a tent make a circus," said the man. "And I'm not having a circus. I just want a straight restaurant with dancing elephants."

"Chairs," said the woman.

"Right," said the man. "We've got eighteen tables now, and four chairs to a table makes seventy-two chairs.

We already have two chairs so I just have to make seventy more. I can't wait to see the whole thing put together. The eighteen tables and the eighteen elephants dancing and the seventy-two people sitting on the chairs in the restaurant."

"And a chef," said the woman. "I can cook for two people but not for seventy-two."

"Right," said the man. "When I advertise for the elephants, I'll put in the ad: Dancing and cooking experience helpful."

"Bookkeeping," said the woman. "After all, it's a business."

"Dancing, cooking and bookkeeping experience," said the man. He put the advertisement in the local newspaper:

Elephants wanted for table work. Must be agile. Dancing, cooking and bookkeeping experience helpful.

Then he went into the woods and cut down four restaurantwood trees and two chairwood trees. He sawed up the wood and he stacked it and he left it to season for a couple of years.

Meanwhile they began to get telephone calls from elephants. The first elephant who called was not agile and he could not dance, cook or keep books. But he was an experienced truck driver.

"I'll hire him," said the man. "If things get slow, we can fill in with long-distance trucking."

"And truck drivers always like a good place to eat, and they tell their friends," said the woman. "So that'll bring in new customers."

The man hired the elephant and went into the
woods and cut down a truckwood tree. He sawed it up
and left the wood to season.

The next elephant who rang them up was a dancing
instructor. The one after that was a cook.

The one after that was a bookkeeper.

All of them were agile.

"That's four," said the man. "Now we only need fourteen more elephants."

"Fifteen," said the woman. "We need nineteen altogether. Eighteen for the tables and one in the kitchen."

Fifteen more elephants rang up. All of them were agile and interested in table work.

"Now we're all set," said the man. "While we're waiting for the wood to season, the elephants can practise their dancing and we'll be in good shape when it's time to open the restaurant."

27

The telephone rang. It was another elephant.

"We've already got nineteen elephants," said the man. "We don't need any more."

"Nineteen is a funny number," said the elephant on the telephone. "With twenty you can call it 'The Twenty-Elephant Restaurant'."

"Are you agile?" said the man.

"No," said the elephant. "But I'm reliable."

"All right," said the man. "You're hired."

The twentieth elephant made road signs for the restaurant. He went out and put up a sign every ten miles on all the roads for a hundred miles in all directions. Every sign told how far it was to:

The
Twenty-
Elephant
Restaurant
~
TRUCKS YES
→ 60 MILE

The twentieth elephant was out putting up signs for two years while the elephants practised dancing. When he got back, there was a line of cars and trucks ten miles long waiting for the restaurant to open.

By then the chairwood and the restaurantwood and
the truckwood were well enough seasoned, so the man
got to work. First he made the seventy chairs.

As soon as the chairs were finished everybody got out of the trucks and cars. Seventy-two of them pulled the chairs up to the tables and sat down. "Where's the restaurant?" they said.

"I'm building it now," said the man.

He started sawing and hammering while everybody watched him. Those who had chairs sat down and watched and those who didn't have chairs stood and watched.

"Don't watch me," said the man. "Watch the elephants."

The eighteen elephant waiters all got up on the tables and started to dance.

"Down in front!" everybody said to the elephants. "Get off the tables, you're blocking our view."

"Don't you want to see us dance?" said the elephants. "We've been practising every day for two years."

"Get down!" everybody shouted. "We can't see what he's doing."

"Nothing goes right for me," said the man. "I start out to have a twenty-elephant restaurant and I wind up being a one-man circus."

"It's only temporary," said the woman. "Don't do any more until we collect admission money and sell some hot dogs."

The twentieth elephant quickly made a sign:

Mr BUILDO
The One-Man Circus!

See Mr Buildo
build a Restavrant
Single-handed!
Admission 50p

Enjoy a hot dog
cooked and served
by dancing
elephants

"You'd better make that 50p daily admission," said the man. "It's going to take me two weeks to build this restaurant."

So they changed the sign and they collected 50p from everybody. Then the elephant chef made hot dogs, and the elephant waiters danced around and sold them.

The man built the restaurant and wired it and put in the plumbing and installed the kitchen. He painted and stained and varnished and he screwed in the light bulbs and hooked up the music. It took him two weeks to finish the restaurant.

Everybody stayed to watch for the whole two weeks, and they paid 50p and ate hot dogs every day.

When the restaurant was finished, he turned on the music and he turned on the sign and it flashed on and off.

Everybody clapped and cheered, and the man bowed. Then everybody went into the restaurant and had a meal.

While they were eating, the man took the truckwood and he built an enormous truck.

"What's that for?" said the woman. "We don't need a truck now. The restaurant is a big success and we won't have to do any long-distance trucking."

"I don't like taking anything for granted any more," said the man.

There were long lines of cars and trucks at the restaurant every day. The elephant chef was cooking and the elephant dancing instructor was working up new routines, the elephant waiters were dancing on the tables before and after every meal and the elephant bookkeeper was adding up big profits. The dancing instructor taught the twentieth elephant to dance too, so everybody was busy all the time.

One evening one of the customers said, "Why
is my cream-of-chicken
soup sliding back and
forth in the bowl?"

The elephant waiter called the man over. The man looked at the table carefully and he checked every leg separately. The table was as steady as a rock. While he was checking the table a customer at another table said, "Why is my jelly quivering like that?"

The man checked the other table. That one too was as steady as a rock. He went to a corner of the restaurant and shifted his weight from one foot to the other. Everything on all the tables wobbled.

"Matchbook?" said the woman.

"No," said the man. "I'm not having that."

He took the restaurant apart and the elephants loaded it into the truck. The man and the woman and all the elephants got in, the truck-driver elephant started the truck and they all drove off.

"Where to?" said the truck-driver elephant.

"Somewhere flat," said the man.

When they found a flat place, the twenty elephants

went out and moved all the road signs so they told
how far it was to the new location. Then they put up
the sign that said:

Mr BUILDO
The One-Man Circus!

See Mr Buildo
build a Restaurant
Single-handed!
Admission DAILY
50p

Enjoy a hot dog
cooked and served
by dancing
elephants

They collected admission money and they
sold hot dogs and the man put the restaurant
together again. Business was good and they
stayed until the restaurant started to wobble.
Then they moved on.

"Maybe there aren't any places that'll stay

flat," said the woman. "Maybe that's just how it is."

"I think maybe you're right," said the man. "Sometimes it's a one-man circus and sometimes it's a twenty-elephant restaurant. And that's life."

"Still," said the elephants, "it's not a bad life."

"No," said the man, "it isn't."

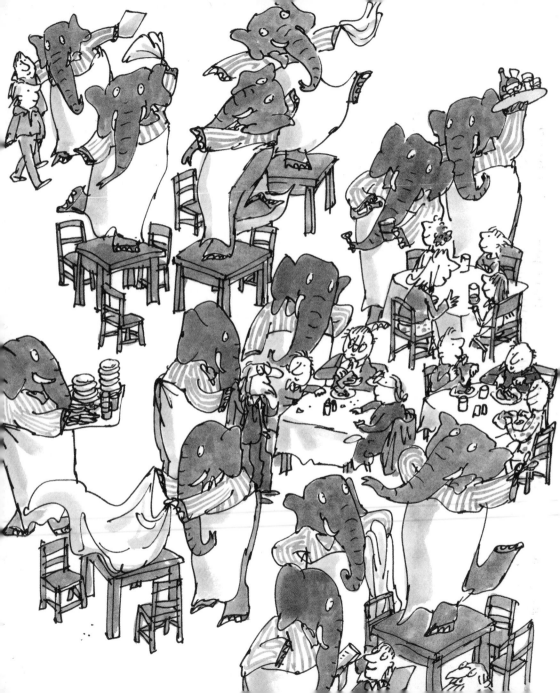